WHY THE POSSUM'S TAIL IS BARE

WHY THE POSSUM'S TAIL IS BARE

and Other North American Indian Nature Tales

collected by James E. Connolly / illustrated by Andrea Adams

Stemmer House

PUBLISHERS, INC.

OWINGS MILLS, MARYLAND

Inquiries should be directed to Stemmer House Publishers, Inc., 2627 Caves Road, Owings Mills, Maryland 21117

Acknowledgments
For permission to include the stories named, we wish to thank the following:
Farrar, Straus and Giroux, Inc. for "This Newly Created World," a Winnebago poem, from *In the Trail of the Wind*, edited by John Bierhorst. Copyright © 1971 by John Bierhorst.
The New York State Education Department and the New York State Museum for "How the Bear Lost Its Tail," from *Myths and Legends of the New York Iroquois* by Harriet Converse.
Akwesasne Notes for "The Hermit Thrush," from *Tales of the Iroquois* by Tehanetorens.
The Smithsonian Institution for "Why the Possum's Tail Is Bare," "How the Rabbit Stole the Otter's Coat," "The Race Between the Crane and the Hummingbird" and "How the Turtle Beat the Rabbit," from *Myths of the Cherokee* by James Mooney.
National Wildlife Federation for "Why the Possum's Tail Is Bare," copyright © 1982, to appear in *Ranger Rick* magazine in May 1985.
Michigan State University Press for "The Broken Wing," from *Schoolcraft's Indian Legends*, edited by Mentor L. Williams.
American Folklore Society for "Rabbit Searches for His Dinner," from *Journal of American Folklore* 28, 1915, "Some Micmac Tales from Cape Breton Island," by Frank G. Speck.
University of Nebraska Press for "Oldman and the Bobcat," from *Blackfoot Lodge Tales* by George Bird Grinnell, Bison Book Edition.
McClelland and Stewart Limited, Toronto, Canada, for "The Origin of the Chickadee" and "The Mallard's Tail," from *Sacred Legends of the Sandy Lake Cree* by Carl Ray and James Stevens.
University of Washington Press for "Coyote in the Cedar Tree," from *Coyote Was Going There*, edited by Jarold Ramsey.

A Barbara Holdridge book

Printed and bound in the United States of America
First printing 1985
Second printing 1986
Third printing 1989
Fourth printing 1992

Library of Congress Cataloging in Publication Data
Connolly, James E. (James Edward), 1949-
    Why the possum's tail is bare, and other North American Indian nature tales.

    "A Barbara Holdridge book."
    Summary: Thirteen tales collected from eight Indian tribes of eastern and western North America, featuring animals and nature lore.
    1. Indian of North America — Legends.   2. Animals — Folklore.   [1. Indians of North America — Legends.   2. Animals — Fiction]   I. Adams, Andrea, ill.   II. Title   III. Title: Why the possum's tail is bare.
E98.F6C69   1985   398.2′08997   84-26871
ISBN 0-88045-069-X HC   ISBN 0-88045-107-6 PB

Colophon
Designed by Barbara Holdridge
Composed in Caslon Book and Caslon Book Italic display type with swash by Brown Composition, Inc., Baltimore, Maryland
Printed on 70-pound Richmond Light Natural Laid Text and bound by Worzalla Printers-Binders, Stevens Point, Wisconsin
Jacket and cover printed by Worzalla Printers-Binders

To Family and Friends

Pleasant it looked,
this newly created world.
Along the entire length and
breadth
of the earth, our grandmother
extended the green reflection
of her covering
and the escaping odors
were pleasant to inhale.

Winnebago Poem

CONTENTS

INTRODUCTION

THE PURPOSE OF THIS COLLECTION OF STORIES is to share with the reader some of the nature tales and myths used by our Native American cultures. These stories were passed on from generation to generation by tribal storytellers and later collected by anthropologists and recorded in numerous journals. Much of the material contained in this book has been revised to effect a consistent narrative prose style.

Stories like these were told to amuse and instruct both adults and children. Tales about the natural world reflected native respect for living things. Animals were given personalities, and the stories served either to teach a moral important to the tribe's values or to relate significant facts about the habits of the animals in the tales. As different tribes came into contact with Europeans, fables that were brought from the Old World were also adapted and incorporated into tribal lore. A tribal storyteller could keep the attention of his audience for hours while relating ancient myths, tribal histories, exciting tales of adventure or stories that explained religious beliefs and customs.

The thirteen stories in this book are taken from the traditions of eight different tribes. Often when the American public visualizes an Indian, the popularized Hollywood warrior who fought Custer and the Seventh Calvary comes to mind. This stereotype should not be considered the "typical" Indian, or even the "typical" Plains Indian. Like the term Indian itself, many of our conceptions concerning the tribes of North America are not reliably authentic. When this continent was explored by Europeans, there were many divergent cultures existing from coast to coast, speaking many languages, practicing many religions and living many lifestyles. Even today there are still well over 100 different tribal languages in use. Anthropologists have spent many years attempting to categorize the Indian peoples by languages, culture groups or geographical areas, but none of the methods used is completely satisfactory because of the diversity from area to area. This volume is simply divided between stories from Eastern tribes and those from Western tribes. The life and customs of these people are described in the following sections.

THE EASTERN WOODLAND TRIBES

The native people of the Eastern forests consisted of two main groups: those who spoke the Algonquian language and those who spoke Iroquois. The tribes in this area practiced agriculture. They planted maize, beans, squash and tobacco in the spring and hunted deer and small game in the fall and winter. Their cultures were adversely affected by European settlement, and in many cases, all that remains to let us know that this land once was occupied by others are the names of places such as Manhattan and Connecticut. There are, however, still groups like the Iroquois of northern New York and Ontario that maintain tribal customs and activities on lands which they have occupied for centuries.

The first two stories are from the Iroquois nation, a confederation of five tribes — the Cayuga, Mohawk, Oneida, Onondaga and Seneca. The Huron and Tuscarora tribes also spoke the same language but were not part of the original "Iroquois League," which was founded sometime before 1500. The story of Hiawatha was the Iroquois tale, greatly altered by Henry Wadsworth Longfellow, of how the confederation came to be. The word "Iroquois" is derived from an Algonquian Indian word meaning "rattlesnake people." It was not exactly a term of endearment, since the Algonquians were enemies of the Iroquois. The Iroquois actually called themselves "Hodenosaune" or "People of the Long Houses." The tribes lived in villages which were protected by walls of logs. Each longhouse had a number of families living in it. The villages were permanent settlements, usually located along the banks of rivers or lakes.

Because they were better organized than most tribal groups, the Iroquois played an important role in the history of the Northeastern states, especially during the French and Indian Wars. They were bitter enemies to French interests in New York State and enabled the British to maintain important trading outposts in the Albany area. Until the early 1800s, the Iroquois were the largest and most powerful tribe in North America. Warfare was an important part of their culture, and status was achieved by bravery and fearlessness in raids against enemies. During the Revolutionary War, most of the Iroquois Confederacy sided with the British. Eventually the success of the colonists caused the Mohawks, Cayugas and Oneidas to leave New York and move to Ontario. The present headquarters for the Iroquois nation is located on Onondaga land south of Syracuse, New York.

The Cherokee spoke a language similar to that of the Iroquois. However, they lived in the Southeast, with over 200 settlements in North Carolina, Virginia, Tennessee, Georgia and Alabama. Early in the 1800s, they began to adopt European agricultural and social practices. They used a republican form of government, built log cabins and raised farm animals. Pressure from advancing settlers led to a treaty in which tribal lands were given to the State of Georgia. The Cherokee were then forced to move west of the Mississippi River. In the winter of 1838, escorted by U.S. Army troops, 14,000 Cherokee were marched forcibly to what is now Oklahoma. Over 4,000 people died of starvation and exposure to cold, and the journey is known by the Cherokee as the "Trail of Tears." During the removal, a number of Cherokee escaped and settled in the Great Smokey Mountains in western North Carolina. They were later able to reacquire 56,000 of the 7 million acres that had been seized from them by the United States government.

The Ojibway, also known as the Chippewa, was a tribe originally located on the upper peninsula of Michigan. From there they expanded the territory they occupied. Members of this tribe now live in parts of Michigan, Minnesota, Montana, North Dakota, Wisconsin, Ontario, Manitoba and Saskatchewan. One of the more populous groups in North America today, this was one of the first tribes to have its myths and legends recorded, a task accomplished by Henry Schoolcraft in the early 1800s. The story called "the Broken Wing" is based on one of the stories that Schoolcraft collected.

The Ojibway culture emphasizes self-reliance and suppression of emotions. Fighting and conflict were rare, and hostility expressed itself in the form of sorcery. Their stories often were about supernatural characters, among whom the one known as Windigo was the most important.

The lives of some Ojibway still revolve around the harvesting of wild rice, which is accomplished with small boats as their ancestors have done for generations. Almost all of the wild rice sold in the United States is produced by them. Today many Ojibway also work in the lumber industry, as well as in fur-trapping and hunting-guide services.

The last story from the Eastern tribes is taken from the Micmac of Canada. These were probably the first North American people to be encountered by Europeans. The Viking stories of Leif Ericson give an account of this group, whose culture was based on fishing off the coast of Nova Scotia, New Brunswick,

Prince Edward Island and Quebec. The Micmac also gathered clams, mussels and bird eggs from spring until fall. In the winter they hunted bear, moose, seal and small game. There are approximately 10,000 Micmac living in Canada, many in cities such as Quebec and Montreal. There are still strong ties to family and friends on tribal land in Nova Scotia and New Brunswick.

THE WESTERN TRIBES

The stories from Western tribal groups, with the exception of the last tale from the Chinook Indians, come from the area of the Great Plains. The tribes that hunted the buffalo on the plains were more nomadic than the forest-living Indians of the East, with less structured tribal organization. Bands within each tribe were linked by friendship, language, marriage and geographic area.

The first story is from the Comanche, who dominated Texas until they were removed to Oklahoma reservations in the mid 1800s. The name that has been used for the tribe, like many in common use today, was not their actual name. They called themselves "Neme-ne" or "People." The word Comanche is from the Ute Indian word for enemy. And the Comanches were enemies of many tribes in the area. They had acquired familiarity with horses from the Spanish during the 1700s and used them to their advantage for warfare against other tribes. They practiced little or no farming and, like the other tribes of the Great Plains, depended on the buffalo for their survival. They also raided neighboring tribes for corn and other provisions.

The Sioux are a linguistic family of tribes made up of a number of branches from different areas in the Midwest and Northeast. The largest branch was the Lakotas. Other tribes that spoke the same or similar languages included the Mandan, Crow, Winnebago, Iowa, Omaha, Osage, Biloxi, Santee and Arkansa. When they were first contacted by Europeans, the Lakotas were living in what is now Minnesota, where they hunted deer, gathered wild rice and caught fish. By 1750, under pressure from the Ojibways who had received rifles and other arms in fur-trading with the French, the Lakotas moved to the Black Hills of South Dakota. The word "Sioux" is another tribal name taken from a word used by one of their enemies. It is a French version of an Ojibway word meaning "Little Snake."

The lifestyle of the Plains Sioux depended on the success of the buffalo hunt. Every summer, isolated bands that had spent the winter sheltered in protected river valleys would gather together for a group hunt. This gathering was also the most important part of the Sioux social, political and religious life. Friendships were renewed, marriages arranged, and the religious ceremony of the Sun Dance performed.

Continued expansion of the Western frontier caused increased conflict between the tribes and new settlers, who began to use larger amounts of traditional hunting land of the Sioux. Gold discoveries in the Black Hills led to the confrontation at Little Bighorn between the Seventh Cavalry and a large band of Sioux and other Plains tribes led by the Oglala Sioux chief, Crazy Horse.

Most of the Sioux tribes were forced onto reservations by the late 1800s. Today the Sioux are one of the most numerous Native American groups, with over 100,000 living in the Dakotas and Montana.

To the north of the Lakota Sioux was the territory of the Blackfoot. This group consists of three tribes, Piegan, Blood and Blackfoot, which all speak a related Algonquian language. They practiced the typical Plains hunting lifestyle. Horses were their wealth, and some families owned hundreds of them. Many Blackfoot starved when the buffalo was hunted close to extinction. Reservation life was not an easy adjustment for them, or in fact for any of the Plains Indians, who lacked any knowledge of farming, and found little satisfaction in a sedentary lifestyle. Some, however, were able to become successful cattlemen. Today a few thousand Blackfoot live on reservations in Montana and Alberta. The majority, however, have left the reservation for other pursuits.

The Cree Indians, like the Blackfoot, spoke a variation of the Algonquian language. This was, other than Sioux and Iroquois, the main spoken language of the tribes of the northern United States and Canada, from the Atlantic Coast to the Rocky Mountains. The Cree were originally a woodland tribe that hunted caribou, moose and other game in the northern forests. During the 1700s, a large number of Cree moved to the plains of Alberta, Saskatchewan and Montana, where they became buffalo hunters like the other Plains Indians. Most Cree now live in villages in Canada, where they work in mining, manufacturing and cattle-raising.

The final story in this volume is taken from one of the tribes of the Pacific Northwest. The tribes that inhabited the Pacific Coast were distinctive in their language, lifestyles and racial features. Their culture can be more closely linked to Eastern Asia than to other North American tribes. Plank houses, straw hats, wooden armor and other cultural traits set them apart.

The Chinook tribe lived along the Columbia River in what is now the state of Washington. They played an important role in controlling trading routes along the coast and into the mountains to the West. Their economy depended upon fishing, especially for salmon. They also made use of sea mammals, shellfish, birds and small game. They did not practice any farming, but gathered wild fruit, berries and roots. The mild winters and abundant food sources of the West Coast gave the Chinook the leisure time to develop complex social systems. The Potlatch Ceremony, in which tribal members gave away canoes, hides, blankets, clothing and houses, was an important part of their social life. There are only a small number of Chinook left in this area. Contact with white settlers and sailors from whaling ships caused them to contract diseases such as smallpox and measles, for which they had no natural immunity. Many thousands died in the early 1800s. A few hundred of the tribe now share reservations with other tribes in Washington and Oregon.

With their differences understood, we can contemplate what these stories and their storytellers had in common: keen observation of nature, desire to teach virtues, and respect for all living things.

Saranac Lake, New York
March 1985

James E. Connolly

HOW THE BEAR LOST ITS TAIL

An Iroquois Folktale

Since the bear is the largest meat-eating animal in North America, and a mother bear with cubs can be a ferocious and intimidating protector of her brood, Indian tribes had a healthy respect for this creature, often depicting it as a sort of "policeman of the woods" in many stories.

Black bears are by far the most numerous of the bear clan found in North America. They eat a varied diet, but mostly grass, berries, fruit, honey, ants and small animals. They would not generally be looking for a meal near water as is depicted in this story, but grizzly bears and Alaskan brown bears both eat a considerable amount of salmon during the spring salmon runs. The bear, which can hear and smell much better than it can see, is taken advantage of by a sly fox who gets a free dinner through his deceit. The fox is one of the most intelligent animals of the forest. Fox often go out of their way to outsmart men and their hunting dogs, leading them on long chases by running in streams, leaping onto fences and going through hollow logs to lose them. They eat much more meat then bears — mainly mice, rats and other small game. Although the fox gets the best of the bear in this tale, the bear is not an unintelligent creature either. It accumulates knowledge from experience, and the older the bear, the wiser it is. Bears do not carry any food to their winter dens, as is depicted in the story. They accumulate a layer of fat and go into a deep sleep, which in warm areas may be only for a few days' duration.

A BEAR, WHO WAS SEARCHING THE FOREST FOR HIS WINTER STORE OF NUTS, had travelled far from his home when he met an aged fox. The fox told him that he had just seen some strange little animals playing by the river not far away. He had seen the animals diving down to a burrow beneath the water, but had not seen them return to the surface again. "Perhaps," he said to the bear, "they are young otter which we could catch for dinner." The fox urged the bear to go with him and try to trick these animals into leaving their hiding place.

The bear, smacking his lips and hanging out his tongue in anticipation of a feast, ran down to the river as quickly as he could. He leaned over the water and, seeing the reflection of his own face, believed it to be one of the animals that the fox had described. So he sat down to watch for its reappearance.

The bear waited for a long time, all the while being encouraged by the fox. At last it dawned on the bear that he might be able to catch the otters with a fishing line. Surely he had the patience to wait all day by the stream and the cunning to watch breathlessly? But he had no line or bait! What was he to do? The artful fox suggested that he could swim to a log that was floating nearby and then use his tail as his fishing line. "Then if you get a bite," explained the fox, "whip the catch over to shore, where I'll protect it for you."

So the unsuspecting bear swam out to the log. There he secured himself and dropped his tail into the water. Now the tail of the bear was very broad, and so long that it reached near the bottom of the river. Soon something shook the tail. As the bear lifted it up, he saw a wriggling little animal. "Not a bird," he thought, "nor a fish, but a juicy otter." He slung it across the water to the waiting fox.

"That's fine!" cried the fox. "Keep up the good work."

Again and again the bear lowered his tail into the water. Whenever the tail shook, he would throw his game to the fox. This continued until a gusty north wind blew its cold breath over the water. The river became quiet and its waves suddenly stretched out as smooth as a blanket. The North Wind had frozen the river solid. The bear, thinking only of his prey, didn't even notice. Nor did he see the crafty fox busily eating the catch. "I don't feel any more nibbles at the bait!" he yelled over to the fox.

The fox, who was caught coughing over a bone, wheezed back, "it's just this bad wind. Wait until it passes over!"

So the bear waited a long time, until it was beginning to get dark. He started to think about the long journey home and all the game that he must carry home as well. So he yelled over to the fox, "How would you like to help me carry my catch home and share in the feast for your troubles?"

But no answer came to his invitation. Again he called over to the fox and still no reply came. So he lifted himself up and began to jump over to shore. He felt a heavy tugging. "The biggest catch yet!" he thought to himself. Pulling as hard as he could, he jumped over to the shore. But his tail was left behind in the frozen water! The North Wind had frozen it there! And the friendly, advising fox was nowhere to be seen. The only thing left was a pile of half-chewed bones.

With a sigh and a half-hearted smile, the tailless bear lifted up his load of honey and lumbered along to his cave for the winter months. To this day, his tailless descendents have never really liked to go fishing.

From an Iroquois myth collected by Harriet Converse, New York State Educational Dept. Bulletin (1908)

THE HERMIT THRUSH

An Iroquois Folktale

Many people feel that the hermit thrush has the most intricate and beautiful song of any North American bird, almost flute-like in its quality. This is the story of how it learned to sing so beautifully. As the story relates, this thrush, a close relation of the robin, is a very shy bird that is seldom seen, thus inspiring its name. It prefers to live in deep evergreen woods in its northern breeding range, and in hardwood forests and thickets when it moves south for the winter.

Different species of birds prefer to sing at particular times of the day. Many birds actively sing at sunrise. The cacophony of singing is called "dawn chorus." As is true of most thrushes, except for the robin which sings both at dawn and sunset, the hermit thrush gives its most vocal performance at sunset.

Bird songs serve a variety of purposes and are particularly associated with the breeding season. Songs serve as a territorial warning to discourage other male birds, attract a mate, and maintain the bond between pairs. Many species of birds need to acquire their typical songs by listening to adult birds of their own species. This is particularly true of birds with elaborate songs such as the hermit thrush. Because of this, local populations of a species often have variations, or regional dialects, in different parts of their ranges. After the breeding seasons, some birds still continue singing, especially in autumn, just prior to migration.

Other sounds that birds make, known as "calls," are not associated with the breeding cycle, but are used for begging, scolding, warning, alarm or aggression.

Some species, such as hummingbirds, have a peculiar method of singing. Wing vibrations and air passing through their feathers produce sounds which serve the same function as songs produced by the syrinx in the windpipe of other species. This "mechanical" song is produced by a number of other birds, including grouse, snipe, woodcock and nighthawks. The drumming of woodpeckers on hollow trees serves the same purpose. The birds that are most vocal are our small perching birds or "passerines." These include thrushes, wrens, warblers, swallows, mockingbirds and a host of others, which collectively are often called "songbirds." Other birds have less singing ability and many of the larger birds, such as vultures, storks and pelicans, make little or no sound at all. They communicate primarily through gestures, display and mechanical means.

17

The idea that small birds "hitchhike" on the back of larger ones is, interestingly, a common misconception. In Europe, it was one of the ways used to explain how small birds were able to fly over large bodies of water such as the Mediterranean Sea. We now know that even small birds do not need a ride from larger eagles or swans, but are able to fly over great distances and even at great heights. Birds regularly fly over such mountain ranges as the Himalayas during migration, and have been recorded at heights of up to 20,000 feet in some instances. Hawks and eagles make use of thermals, currents of warm air, to soar to high altitudes. Even small birds take advantage of prevailing winds at high altitudes, in the same way that airplanes use jet streams to conserve fuel.

LONG AGO, THE BIRDS HAD NO SONGS. ONLY MAN COULD SING, and every morning men would greet the rising sun with a song. The birds, as they were flying by, would often stop and listen to the beautiful songs of men. In their hearts they wished that they too could sing in the same way.

One day, the Good Spirit visited the Earth. He walked around inspecting all the things He had created. As He walked through the forest, He noticed that there was a great silence. Something seemed to be missing. As He pondered this, the sun sank behind the western hills. From the direction of the river, where there was an Indian village, there sounded the deep rich tones of an Indian drum, followed by the sacred chanting of the sunset song. The Good Spirit listened and He was pleased by the sound. He looked around and noticed that the birds were also listening to the singing.

"That is what is missing!" said the Good Spirit. "Birds should also have songs."

The next day, the Good Spirit called all of the birds together for a great council. From near and far they came. The sky was filled with flying birds. The trees and bushes bent to the earth under the weight of so many. On the Council Rock sat the Good Spirit. He waited until all of the birds had perched and become quiet. Then the Good Spirit spoke.

"Would you like to have songs, songs such as the people sing?"

With one voice, the birds all chirped, "Yes! Yes!"

"Very well," He said. "Tomorrow when the sun rises in the East, you are all to fly up into the sky. You are to fly as high as you can. When you can fly no higher, you will find your song. That bird who flies the highest will have the most beautiful song of all the birds." Saying these words, the Good Spirit vanished.

Next morning, long before sunrise, the birds were ready. There were birds everywhere. The Earth was covered with them. There was great excitement. However, one little bird was very unhappy. He was the little brown thrush. Perched beside him was the great eagle. As the little bird gazed at the eagle, he thought, "What chance have I to compete with this great bird? I am so little and Eagle is so large. I will never be able to fly as high as he."

As he was thinking this, an idea entered his mind.

"Eagle is so excited that he will not notice if I hide myself somewhere in his feathers!" With this thought in mind, the brown bird flew like a flash and quickly hid under the great bird's back feathers. Eagle didn't even notice, because he was only thinking about winning: "With my great wings, I will surely win," he said.

The sun finally looked over the eastern mountains and with a great roar of wings, the many birds took off. The air was so full of flying birds that for a time the sky was dark. Their bodies covered the face of the sun. For a long time, the birds flew upward. Finally, the smaller, weaker birds began to tire. The little hummingbird was the first to give up. His little wings beat the air so hard that to this day one can, if one listens, hear his humming wings. His little squeaking call says, "Wait for me, wait for me." It is a very plain song, for he was not able to fly very high.

The fat cowbird was the next to give up. As he floated down, he listened and heard his song, a very common one. Other birds weakened, and while flying eastward, listened and learned their songs.

At last, the sun was at the end of the Earth. The night sky began to darken everything. By this time, there were only a few birds left. They were the larger, strong-winged birds: the eagle, hawk, owl, buzzard and loon. All night, the birds flew up, never even stopping for a rest.

When the sun rose next morning, only the eagle, chief of all birds, was left. He was still going strong. Finally, he began to tire. With a look of triumph, for there were no other birds in sight, the tired eagle began to glide earthward. The little thrush, riding under the feathers of the great eagle, had been asleep all this time. When the eagle started back to Earth, little Thrush awoke. He hopped off the eagle's head and began to fly upward. Eagle saw him go and glared with anger at him, but was powerless to stop him, for he was completely exhausted.

The little thrush flew up and up. He soon came to a hole in the sky. He found himself in a beautiful country, the Land of Good Spirits. As he entered the Spirit World, he heard a beautiful song. He stayed there in heaven for a while, learning this song. When he had learned it completely, he left the Land of Good Spirits and flew back toward Earth.

Thrush could hardly wait to reach the Earth. He was anxious to show off his beautiful song. As he neared the ground, he glanced down at the Council Rock. There sat all the birds, and on the Council rock, glaring up at him, was Eagle. All of the birds were very silent as they waited for Thrush to come down.

Suddenly the feeling of glory left the little thrush, and he felt ashamed. He knew that he had cheated to get his beautiful song. He also feared Eagle, who might get even with him for stealing a free ride. He flew in silence to the deep woods, and in shame, hid under the branches of the largest tree. He was so ashamed that he wanted no one to see him.

There you will find him today. Never does the hermit thrush come out into the open. He is still ashamed because he cheated. Sometimes, however, he cannot restrain himself and he must sing his beautiful song. When he does this, the other birds cease their singing. They know that the song of the Hermit Thrush, the song from the Spirit World, is the most beautiful of all. That is why the song of this shy bird causes the sun to shine in the heart of anyone who is lucky enough to hear it in the deep forest.

An Iroquois legend from *Tales of the Iroquois*, by Tehanetorens, Akwesasne Notes, Rooseveltown, N.Y. (1976)

WHY THE POSSUM'S TAIL IS BARE

A Cherokee Folktale

Many tales collected from Indian sources revolve around a cunning and deceitful rabbit, constantly getting into mischief and playing tricks on other animals, such as the poor possum here.

The possum is the only North American marsupial or pouched mammal, which makes it a distant relative of Australian kangaroos, koalas and bandicoots. As the story relates, the tail has little hair and appears scaly. The possum can use his tail as an "extra" hand, carrying leaves in it for its den and assisting in climbing trees. When cornered by a predator, such as a fox or coyote, the possum will often become limp and roll over on its back as if it were dead. This behavior is responsible for the term "playing possum." Some, however, believe that the animal, which has a very tiny brain, has actually gone into shock from fright.

The cricket was known as the "barber" by some tribes. This musical insect has special structures called a file and a scraper on its wings, with which the male cricket produces songs in summer. Perhaps the cricket in the story uses these as his barber "tools," or else employs his biting mouth-parts to give the possum a trim.

THE POSSUM USED TO HAVE A LONG, BUSHY TAIL, AND WAS SO PROUD OF IT that he combed it out every morning and sang about it all the time. The rabbit, who had no tail, became very jealous and made up his mind to play a trick on the possum.

There was to be a great council and a dance at which all the animals were to be present. It was the rabbit's business to send out the news, so as he was passing the possum's place he stopped to ask him if he intended to be there. The possum said he would come if he could have a special seat, "because I have such a handsome tail that I ought to sit where everyone can see me." The rabbit promised to attend to it and to send someone to comb and dress the possum's tail as well. The possum was very much pleased and agreed to come.

The rabbit then went over to see the cricket, who is such an expert haircutter that the Indians call him the barber. Rabbit told him to go the next morning and prepare the possum's tail for the upcoming dance. He told the cricket just what to do and then went on about some other mischief.

In the morning, the cricket went to the possum's house saying, "I've come to get you ready for the dance." So the possum stretched himself out and shut his eyes while the cricket combed out his tail and

wrapped a red string around it to keep it smooth until night. But all the time, as he wound the string around, he was clipping off the hair close to the roots, and the possum never knew it.

When it was night, the possum went to the meetinghouse where the dance was to be and found the best seat ready for him, just as the rabbit had promised. When his turn came in the dance, he loosened the string from his tail and stepped into the middle of the floor. The drummers began to drum and the possum began to sing, "See my beautiful tail." Everybody shouted and he danced around the circle and sang again, "See what a fine color it has." They shouted again and he danced around another time, singing, "See how it sweeps the ground." The animals shouted more loudly than ever, and the possum was delighted. He danced around again and sang, "See how fine the fur is." Then everybody laughed so long that the possum wondered what they meant by it. He looked around the circle of animals and they were all laughing at him. Then he looked down at his beautiful tail and saw that there was not a hair left upon it; it was as bare as the tail of a lizard. He was so astonished and ashamed that he could not say a word, but rolled over helpless on the ground and grinned, as the possum does to this very day when taken by surprise.

From a Cherokee myth collected by James Mooney, Bureau of American Ethnology, 19th Annual Report (1900)

HOW THE RABBIT STOLE THE OTTER'S COAT

A Cherokee Folktale

Again we see rabbit up to his usual tricks. Perhaps these stories arise from the observation that rabbits are always being chased by larger animals, almost as if they were mad at the rabbits for something. Rabbits are an important prey for a host of animals, including coyotes, fox, weasel, mink, bobcat, owls and hawks. Their main defense is their speed, up to 20 MPH for the cottontail rabbit, and their ability to change direction and run a zig-zag escape route. Their first leap can be up to 15 feet, but they first try to remain motionless in the hope of not being found.

It is understandable that the rabbit in this story is jealous of the beautiful fur of the otter, which is also valued by people to make coats. Otters spend most of their time in the water of streams and lakes. They are skilled in catching fish, moving their slender bodies through the water and propelling themselves with webbed toes. The otter is also known for its playfulness, often chasing objects it drops into the water, such as shells and rocks, or sliding down snow banks, one after another. Sliding is a typical movement used by the otter to move quickly over snow and ice.

ALL THE ANIMALS OF THE FOREST ARE OF DIFFERENT SIZES AND WEAR COATS OF various colors and patterns. Some wear long fur and others wear short. Some have rings on their tails, and some have no tails at all. Some have coats of brown, others of black or yellow. They are always disputing about their good looks and once, many years ago, they agreed to hold a council to decide who had the finest coat.

They had heard a great deal about Otter, who lived so far up the creek that he seldom came down to visit the other animals. It was said that he had the finest coat of all, but no one knew just what it was like, because it was a long time since anyone had seen him. They did not even know exactly where he lived — only the general direction. But they knew he would come to the council when the word got out.

Now Rabbit wanted the prize for himself, so when it began to look as if it might go to the otter he thought of a plan to cheat him out of it. He asked a few sly questions until he learned what trail the otter would take to get to the council place. Then, without saying anything, he went on ahead and after four days travel he met Otter, whom he knew at once by his beautiful coat of soft dark-brown fur. The otter was glad to see him and asked him where he was going. "Oh," said the rabbit, "the animals sent me to bring you to the council. Since you live so far away they were afraid you might not know the way." The otter thanked him, and they went on together.

They traveled all day toward the council ground. At night Rabbit selected the camping place, as the otter was a stranger in that part of the country. They cut down bushes for beds and fixed everything to protect themselves from possible danger. The next morning they started on again. In the afternoon the rabbit began to pick up wood and bark as they went along and to load it on his back. When Otter asked what this was for, Rabbit said it was to make a fire when they camped that night. After a while, when it was near sunset, they stopped and made their camp.

When supper was over, the rabbit got a stick and shaved it down to a paddle. The otter wondered and asked again what that was for. "I have good dreams when I sleep with a paddle under my head," said Rabbit.

When the paddle was finished, the rabbit began to cut away the bushes in order to make a clear path down to the river. The otter wondered more and more and wanted to know what this meant.

Said Rabbit, "This place is called Di'tataski'yi — The Place Where It Rains Fire. Sometimes it rains fire here, and the sky looks a little that way tonight. You go to sleep and I'll sit up and watch, and if the fire does come, as soon as you hear me shout, you run and jump into the river. Better hang your coat on a limb over there, so it won't get burned up."

The otter did as he was told, and they both curled up to go to sleep, but Rabbit stayed awake. After a while the fire burned down to red coals. Rabbit called but Otter was fast asleep and gave no answer. In a little while he called again, but the otter never stirred. Then Rabbit filled the paddle with hot coals and threw them up in the air and shouted, "It's raining fire! It's raining fire!"

The hot coals fell all around the otter and he jumped up. "To the water!" cried the rabbit, and the otter ran and jumped into the river. And he has lived in the water ever since.

Rabbit took Otter's coat and put it on, leaving his own instead, and went on to the council. All the

animals were there, everyone looking out for the otter. At last they saw him in the distance, and they said to one another, "Otter is coming!" They sent one of the small animals to show him the best seat. They were all glad to see him and went up in turn to welcome him, but the otter kept his head down with one paw over his face. They wondered why he was so bashful, until the bear came up and pulled the paw away. There was the rabbit with his split nose. He sprang up and started to run, when the bear struck at him and pulled his tail off. Rabbit, however, was too quick for them and got away.

From a Cherokee myth collected by James Mooney, Bureau of American Ethnology, 19th Annual Report (1900)

THE RACE BETWEEN THE CRANE AND THE HUMMINGBIRD

A Cherokee Folktale

This story matches the smallest and largest birds against each other in a race to see who will marry a beautiful wood duck. The scientific name for the wood duck (Aix sponsa) literally means "bride" or "promised one." The wood duck does look as though it has been prepared for a wedding, being the most brightly colored of any waterfowl found in North America. As with most birds, however, it is the male which has the more beautiful plumage. Both the male and female have feathers forming a flowing crest over their heads and colorful iridescent wings. The display of their many colors is important in pair-formation during the nesting season. These are the only North American perching ducks. Unlike other waterfowl, they nest in tree cavities and forage for acorns and nuts on the forest floor. Although the species was on the verge of extinction earlier in this century, the placement of man-made nest boxes in suitable breeding areas has allowed it to recover.

Anyone would think that a race between a crane and a hummingbird would be won easily by the hummingbird, who can so often be seen darting quickly among flowers, collecting nectar. It is one of the most agile of all birds, and not only can hover, but can even fly backwards. As ungainly as a crane looks, however, it can actually fly faster than a hummingbird and can reach 60 MPH with a good tailwind. Moreover, as the story suggests, hummingbirds are not generally found flying in the evening. Their metabolism is so high that their heartbeat and breathing actually slow down when they are resting at night. This allows them to conserve energy. How these small birds are able to migrate as far as Central America and back every year is a mystery!

If it is any consolation for the wood duck, her disappointment at the crane's victory should be tempered by the fact that male cranes assist in incubating their mates' eggs and rearing the young, while male hummingbirds take no part in domestic duties.

A HUMMINGBIRD AND A CRANE WERE BOTH IN LOVE WITH a beautiful wood duck. She preferred the hummingbird, who was as handsome as the crane was awkward. But the crane was so persistent that in order to get rid of him she finally told him that he must challenge Hummingbird to a race, and she would marry the winner. Hummingbird was so swift, almost like a flash of lightning, and Crane so slow and heavy, that she felt sure the hummingbird would win. But she did not know that the crane could fly all night.

They agreed to start from the nest of the wood duck, which was in a hollow of a tree in the forest.

They would fly from there to the ocean, which was many days' travel from where they were, and then return to the starting point. The one that returned first would be the winner.

At the word "Start!" Hummingbird darted off like an arrow and was out of sight in a moment, leaving Crane to follow slowly behind. He flew all day, and when evening came, he stopped to roost for the night. By this time he was far ahead. But Crane flew steadily all night long, passing Hummingbird soon after midnight. He kept going until about dawn, when he rested by a small creek.

Hummingbird woke up in the morning and flew on again, thinking how easily he would win the race, until he reached the creek where Crane had been resting. There he saw Crane spearing small fish with his long bill and enjoying a leisurely breakfast. He then flew swiftly out of sight and again left Crane far behind.

Crane finished his breakfast and started on, and when evening came he kept on as he had before. This time it was hardly midnight when he passed Hummingbird, asleep on a small limb once more, and in the morning he had finished his breakfast before Hummingbird was in sight. The next day he gained a little more, and on the fourth day he was spearing fish for lunch when Hummingbird passed him. On the fifth and sixth days it was late in the afternoon before Hummingbird caught up, and on the morning of the seventh day, Crane was a whole night's travel ahead. He took his time at breakfast and preened his feathers, since he was nearing the finish line and wanted to look as elegant as he could. When Hummingbird arrived in the afternoon, he found he had lost the race. Wood Duck was very disappointed, but kept her promise to marry the winner.

From a Cherokee myth collected by James Mooney, Bureau of American Ethnology, 19th Annual Report (1900)

HOW THE TURTLE BEAT THE RABBIT

A Cherokee Folktale

Indian storytellers often used a tale to instruct on what was considered improper behavior, such as boastfulness.

The turtles in this story are spotted turtles, which can be found in swamps and marshes in the eastern part of the United States. If the rabbit had been a better observer, he not only could have noticed that he was racing a family of turtles, he could even have told the boys from the girls. The number of spots varies with age, and males of this species have longer tails and darker markings around the jaws.

The turtle is a sacred animal — referred to as "Mother Turtle" — among most North American tribes, because in religious myths about creation, all animals first appeared on the back of a huge turtle, floating in an immense ocean that existed before anything else on earth.

THE RABBIT WAS A GREAT RUNNER, AND EVERYBODY KNEW IT. NO ONE thought the turtle anything but a slow traveler, but he was a great warrior and very boastful, and the two were always disputing about their speed. At last they agreed to decide the matter by a race. They fixed the day and the starting place and arranged to run across four mountain ridges. The one who reached the last ridge first would be the winner.

Rabbit felt so sure of victory that he said to Turtle, "You know you can't run. You can never win the race, so I'll give you a headstart to the first ridge and then you'll have only three to cross while I will have to go over four."

The turtle said that would be all right. They then both returned to their lodges for the night. Turtle, however, sent for his turtle friends and family, telling them that he needed their help.

"I know that I cannot outrun the rabbit, but I am tired of his always boasting about his great speed. It is time someone taught him a little humility. Come listen to my plan."

All his friends agreed to help out. When the day came, all the animals were there to see the race. The rabbit was at the starting point, but the turtle had already gone ahead toward the first ridge, as had

been agreed to earlier. The rabbit started off with a roar from all the crowd as he sprang into action. He started off with long jumps and soon was climbing the first ridge, expecting to win the race before the turtle could get down the other side. But before he got up the mountain, he saw Turtle go over the next ridge ahead of him.

Rabbit ran on. When he reached the top he looked all around, but he could not see the turtle because of the long grass below. He kept going down the mountain and climbed the second ridge, but when he looked up again there was Turtle just going over the top. Now he was both surprised and angry. He began making his longest leaps to catch up, but when he got to the top of the ridge, there was the turtle away in front going over the third ridge.

The rabbit was getting tired now and nearly out of breath, but he kept on down the mountain and up the other ridge until he got to the top. And he was just in time to see Turtle cross the fourth ridge and win the race!

The rabbit could not make another jump, but fell over on the ground, as the rabbit does ever since when he is too tired to run anymore. A ribbon was given to the turtle for winning the race and all the animals wondered how he could win against the rabbit. The turtle wasn't about to tell either. It was easy because all the turtle's family and friends looked just alike, and he had simply had one of them climb to each ridge before the race began. They then waited until the rabbit came in sight before hiding themselves in the long grass. That is how the turtle taught Rabbit not to be too boastful.

From a Cherokee story collected by James Mooney, Bureau of American Ethnology, 19th Annual Report (1900)

THE BROKEN WING

A Chippewa Folkstory

The birds in this tale are peregrine falcons, one of the largest groups of the falcon family, and the fastest flyers of all birds. They attack other birds in the air, diving from above and reaching speeds of up to 200 mph. In recent years the use of the insecticide DDT hampered the peregrine's ability to breed and eliminated it from most of its former range. However, scientists have been able to release birds bred in captivity back to the wild, and the peregrine falcon is slowly being restored. These birds still face danger from great horned owls, which sometimes attack their nests and kill the young falcons.

This story of the broken wing emphasizes the concept of cooperation and mutual aid. It describes how young falcons spend a winter in search of food which they bring back to their injured brother. Actually cooperation among birds of prey such as hawks and falcons is not found in nature. However, the mating and nesting instinct does allow birds, which may normally be solitary hunters, to cooperate in feeding and caring for the young nestlings. Few species of birds leave the nest without a parent to protect them. The young need to practice how to fly, avoid danger and find food. Falcon parents teach the young how to hunt by holding game in their talons and allowing the young birds to practice striking at the game in mid-air. Once the necessary skills for survival are mastered, the fledgling birds are on their own and soon begin their migration.

THERE WERE SIX YOUNG FALCONS LIVING IN A NEST, ALL BUT ONE of whom had not yet been taught to hunt by their parents. Both of their parents had been shot by hunters and the oldest bird was trying to feed the others until they could hunt for themselves. He was the only one with feathers and therefore the only one that was able even to leave the nest. He had assumed the duties of their parents, stilling their cries and providing them with food.

One day, by an unlucky chance, he injured a wing while pouncing on a rabbit. He was able to get back to the nest area, but knew that he wasn't able to fly very far. The other falcons were a little bigger and stouter than earlier and were now able to do their own hunting.

"Brothers," said the injured falcon, "an accident has made it impossible for me to fly. It is now time for you to move to the south so that you will be able to survive the cold of winter. Go now to a place where it is warmer and food is plentiful. Winter is coming fast and you cannot stay here. It is better that I alone should die than for all of us to suffer because of my accident."

"No! No!" the other falcons screamed. "We will not leave you. We will share this suffering together. We will take care of you just as you cared for us when we were unable to get our own food. If the weather kills you, it will kill us. You have been like both mother and father to us and we shall live or die with you."

They all sought out a hollow tree where they spent the winter. Before the bad weather had come, they had tried to store up as much food as they could. They decided that two of them should head south, while the others remained to feed and protect the wounded falcon. This is how they spent the winter, feeding on such game as they could find. They hunted especially hard on those days when the sun was uncovered by clouds and the wind did not blow so hard. It was a harsh winter, but nonetheless they survived by working hard and helping each other to hunt.

As spring came, they came out of their hiding place to perch once again on the branches of trees. Game was once again plentiful, but the youngest falcon was having much difficulty finding food. He always came back without anything. At last the older bird spoke up.

"What is the reason for your bad luck in hunting, Little One?" he said.

"It is not my small size, for I am as fast as any of you and even quicker at following dodging rabbits," he replied. "But every time I go out, just as I get to the woods, a large owl robs me of my prey."

"Well, don't worry, my brother," said the oldest falcon, "Now that I have my strength back, I will go out with you tomorrow and we will do something about this."

The next day they both went out to hunt together. Little Falcon soon pounced on a duck that was swimming on a lake.

"Well done!" thought his brother, who was watching closely.

Just as the small falcon was about to land with his prize, up came a great horned owl from a tree and dove at Little Falcon. Now the falcon can fly much faster than an owl, but since Little Falcon had game in his talons, he was slowed down and was forced to drop the game for the larger owl. But his larger brother had seen everything that happened, flew over and grabbed the owl on each side of his body with his sharp

talons. The older falcon carried the owl back to the nest.

Little Falcon was very happy. He followed his brother closely as they returned to the nest. He flew in the owl's face and wanted to tear out his eyes.

"Easy," said the older bird, "do not be so angry, for the owl was just trying to get food as we were. This will be a lesson to Owl and he will learn not to terrorize our kind any longer."

He then told the owl what kinds of herbs would cure his wounds and made him promise that he would no longer harass the falcon clan.

"Thank you for your mercy," said Owl. "I will remember your words from now on and will always keep from bothering your kind."

Ever since that day it has been the habit of Owl never to hunt during the day, which is the time of the falcon to hunt. The owls only come out of their nests when the evening darkness covers the forest and they cannot be seen.

A few days later, the two nestmates of the other falcons returned from the south after spending the winter there, and they were all happily reunited. Each one chose a mate and flew off to build new nests. The cold winds of winter had stopped, the ice had melted, the streams were full of fish, and the forest was turning green.

Adapted from *Algic Researches, Indian Tales and Legends* by Henry R. Schoolcraft, Harper Brothers, New York (1839); reprinted as *Schoolcraft's Indian Legends*, edited by Mentor L. Williams, Michigan State University Press, East Lansing (1956)

RABBIT SEARCHES FOR HIS DINNER

A Micmac Folkstory

This tale relates how the mischievous rabbit foolishly wished to be able to hunt and eat food as both the otter and woodpecker do. It reminds us that all animals, including man, have physical traits which ensure survival and the ability to secure food and shelter. The otter has the ability to close his ears and nose when it dives under water in pursuit of fish. The woodpecker's beak is perfectly suited for drilling away on trees in search of insects.

A rabbit's search for food is not difficult and it has no special adaptations for finding food, which is always abundant and close at hand. Rabbits eat grasses during the summer and tree bark and twigs in winter. Their most important physical attributes are their large ears that help them hear enemies, and the long legs and feet which help them escape. Even though food is abundant, life is not easy for wild rabbits. In fact, very few live beyond one year, since they are helpless, easy prey for many animals. Their survival is based on an amazing ability to breed. Females usually have four to five litters of young in a year and can have up to 35 young during that time. A single pair might thus produce 350,000 "relatives" in a single year if it were not for animals and human hunters, serving to keep their population under control.

OTTER AND RABBIT LIVED WITH THEIR WIVES NOT TOO FAR FROM EACH OTHER. One day Rabbit started out and wandered over to visit Otter at his den.

"How are you doing today?" Rabbit asked his friend.

"Fine," said Otter, "and I am glad you are here for I am about to go find some food for dinner and you will be able to eat here with me and my wife."

So Otter, followed by Rabbit, went out to the pond that was close by his home. He jumped right in, and within just a few minutes, had caught a nice long string of eels. Rabbit was amazed at how quickly Otter had caught his food and was a little bit jealous of him. He thought foolishly that he could catch fish as easily as Otter.

They both went back inside the den and Otter and his wife prepared the eels to eat. After a hardy meal in which Rabbit ate as much as he could fit into his stomach, they said their farewells. "You must come over for dinner tomorrow so that I can return your hospitality," said Rabbit. "I too will prepare some fish in your honor."

The next day Otter went over to Rabbit's camp. When he arrived, Rabbit told his wife to hang the pot over the fire to start boiling some water.

"You wait here while I go out to gather some food," said Rabbit to his wife.

Then Rabbit went out to the pond, just as Otter had done, and dove in to catch some eels. But he could not get anything, not even a fish, and he was unable to stay down under the water no matter how hard he tried. He kept coming up sputtering and choking after only a few seconds under the water.

After a while, Otter went out to see what was wrong. Then he heard, "Cough, cough! Wheeeze!"

There was Rabbit, just about drowning and trying to get to shore. Otter jumped in and hauled him out of the pond.

"What's the matter with you?" asked Otter. "What are you doing trying to swim around the pond when you don't even know how to swim?"

"I was trying to get something to eat," said Rabbit.

"If that's what you wanted you should have called me," replied Otter, as he laughed heartily.

Then Otter jumped into the pond and pulled out a few fish and they both went back to Rabbit's den to eat. Afterwards Otter thanked Rabbit for inviting him over and then went home.

The next day Rabbit started out to visit Woodpecker, who lived in the woods in a big hole that he had carved into a tree with his sharp beak. When Rabbit reached Woodpecker's nest, Rabbit found him there with his wife and children.

"Come on in," said Woodpecker to Rabbit. "You can eat with us."

"We have no food right now," said Woodpecker's wife. "You will have to go out and gather some grubs."

Woodpecker then flew out to a dead tree nearby and began to chisel at it, knocking wood chips this way and that. He used his beak to pick up a bunch of insects he found burrowing in the dead wood, and flew

back to the nest hole. They all had dinner and a large portion was eaten by Woodpecker's children, who kept their mouths open and begged for more.

Rabbit had watched how Woodpecker had obtained his meal and decided to invite him over for dinner the next day. You would have thought he had learned his lesson by now, but no. He thought that he could accomplish anything that the other animals could do.

The next day Woodpecker went over to visit Rabbit. When he arrived, Rabbit asked his wife to hang up their pot on the fire to prepare their dinner.

"But we have nothing to cook," she said.

So Rabbit went outside to gather some food. He saw a dead tree and went over to it. He knew there were a whole lot of bugs in it and he began to peck at the trunk just as he had seen Woodpecker do. Of course, he didn't get very far.

"Oh!" he said. "This hurts a lot. I didn't think the dead wood would be this hard!"

After waiting some time, Woodpecker began to get curious about where Rabbit had gone. He went outside and began to fly around, looking for his host. It wasn't long before he found Rabbit, sitting by the dead tree and rubbing his nose, which was all flattened and split in two from trying to break into the wood.

Woodpecker began to laugh until he almost fell over.

"You are the silliest animal in the forest," he said to Rabbit. "You try to do things that you are incapable of doing and you always get yourself in trouble for it. If you want to imitate others, make sure that you copy others of your tribe instead of all the other animals."

Woodpecker flew off and let out a long laugh, as he still does today when he sees foolish people near his home. Maybe you have heard his laughing in the forest. Ever since that time the foolish Rabbit has had a flat nose split in two.

Adapted from *Some Micmac Tales from Cape Breton Island* by Frank G. Speck, American Folklore Society, *Journal of American Folklore*, Volume 28 (1915)

HOW THE RABBIT LOST ITS TAIL

A Sioux Folkstory

The supernatural hero of this story is Wakan-Tanka. Wakan is the Sioux term for the miraculous and mysterious. Tribal storytellers related tales of the world before man was created, when animals could talk with each other and the world was inhabited by giants and powerful beings. Wakan-Tanka named the animals and the stars and taught men how to hunt and fish. He also taught man how to recognize the different plants that were used for medicine and food.

In this story Wakan-Tanka helps Rabbit stay out of trouble until he gets into one too many predicaments. Rabbits found in the Western prairies could either be a variety of cottontail or one of the hares, either a blacktail or whitetail jackrabbit. Hares are a different species from rabbits, with longer ears and legs. They are built for speed, and are better able to survive in the open areas of the plains, where there is generally less cover. They can outrun all predators and reach speeds up to 40 mph.

Rabbit finally ends up without the help of his powerful friend when he begins playing a test of strength with some wolves. Since wolves would normally make a good meal of a rabbit, he is lucky just to have lost his tail. The story explains why rabbits and hares are constantly on the alert for trouble. In order to survive, they can no longer take the kind of bold chances ventured by the rabbit in this story.

ONCE THERE WAS A YOUNG RABBIT WHO WAS CONTINUALLY GETTING INTO all kinds of trouble. But this rabbit had a powerful friend named Wakan-Tanka, who would get him out of his constant scrapes. Wakan-Tanka was a powerful medicine man, who could change himself into any kind of animal or bird, or into cloud, thunder or lightning. In fact, he could change himself into anything at all.

After Rabbit had attained his full growth, he wanted to travel around and see something of the world. When he told Wakan-Tanka what he wanted to do, Wakan-Tanka said, "Now, Rabbit, you are very mischievous, so be very careful, and keep out of trouble as much as possible. In case you get into any serious trouble, and can't get out by yourself, just call on me for assistance. No matter where you are, I will come to you."

So Rabbit started out. On the first day he came to a very large house, outside of which there stood a very high pine tree. The tree was so high that Rabbit could hardly see to the top. In front of the door to the house, there was an enormous stool. And on the stool there was a very large giant who was fast asleep.

Rabbit had his bow and arrows with him. Taking an arrow from his quiver, he said to himself, "I want to see just how big this man is, so I guess I will wake him up."

He moved over to one side, and taking aim, shot the giant on the nose. Now this arrow just stung the giant, who jumped up, crying, "Who had the nerve to shoot me on the nose?"

"I did," said Rabbit.

The giant, hearing a voice, looked all around, but saw nothing, until he looked down at the house, and there sat Rabbit.

"I was getting hungry this morning and looking for a good meal," said the giant, "and all that I can find is this small little toothful."

"You won't make a toothful out of me," said Rabbit. "I'm as strong as you even though I'm little."

"We will see," said the giant. He went into his house and came out, carrying a hammer that weighed many tons.

"Now, Mr. Rabbit," said he, "we will see who is stronger. We will find out which one of us can throw this hammer over the top of that pine tree."

"Get something harder to do," said Rabbit, wondering how he would get out of this mess.

"Well, we will try this first," said the giant.

With that he grasped the hammer in both hands, swung it three times around his head and sent it spinning through the air. Up, up it went, skimming the top of the tree. It came down again, shaking the ground and burying itself deep in the earth.

"Now," said the giant, "if you don't accomplish this same feat, I am going to swallow you in one mouthful."

Rabbit took a deep breath and said, "I always sing before I do a feat of strength."

So he started to sing, but what he was really doing was calling to Wakan-Tanka, his friend. As he

sang, a small black cloud apeared in the sky, moving towards them very quickly. Rabbit knew that Wakan-Tanka had come to help. He went over to the hammer and pulled it out of the ground with his tiny paws. But it was really Wakan-Tanka lifting the huge weight.

"Watch this!" he cried, and up into the air shot the hammer until it could no longer be seen. After five minutes it came down again and landed right on top of the giant's house. The giant was amazed.

"'You are stronger than I am," he said. "Please do not harm me. Continue on your journey and I will never try to harm you."

Rabbit waved and continued on towards the west. The next day, while passing through a deep forest, he thought he heard someone moaning, as though in pain. He stopped and listened. The wind started to blow and the moaning grew louder. Rabbit followed the direction of the sound and came upon a man tied up between two limbs of a tree.

The man had been placed there as a punishment for evil deeds. But he did not tell this to Rabbit because the only way that he might be set free was to talk someone into taking his place.

"Hello there, young Rabbit," he said as pleasantly as he could. "It sure is lucky that you came along when you did. I am preparing these trees to harvest maple syrup and I need help to make their bark more pliable. I am very tired. Will you be willing to take over for me for awhile?"

"I'd be very glad to help you," said Rabbit.

As soon as Rabbit untied the man and took his place, he realized that something was wrong. There was no way he could get down and the limbs were pulling on his arms and causing great pain. The man began to run off into the forest.

"Where are you going?" cried Rabbit.

"Don't worry about that," said the man, who disappeared into the woods.

"Here I am again in another jam," thought Rabbit. "I will have to call Wakan-Tanka for help." And he began to sing as before for his friend. Again the cloud appeared in the sky and Rabbit knew that Wakan-Tanka was there.

"Help me, Wakan-Tanka, for a man played a trick on me and now I am tied to these trees." Rabbit pointed in the direction taken by the man. Wakan-Tanka flew over the tops of the trees, found the man, and brought him back. He tied him back in his place among the leaves and made the wind blow as punishment for his trickery.

Then he said to Rabbit, "I want you to be more careful in the future. I can't be coming to your rescue all the time. Yesterday I had to come 500 miles to keep a giant from eating you and today you're even in more trouble. How can you be so foolish?"

"I will try to do better from now on," said Rabbit. "I have learned my lesson."

A number of days passed and Rabbit stayed out of trouble. But it wasn't long before he got into more mischief. He was traveling along the banks of a small river when he came upon a little log hut. Rabbit was wondering who could be living there when the door slowly opened and an old man appeared in the doorway. He was carrying a water pail in one hand, and in the other he held a string which was fastened to the inside of the house. He kept hold of the string and walked slowly down to the river. When he got to the water, he stooped down and dipped the pail into it and returned to the house, still holding the string to find his way. Rabbit could tell from this that the old man was blind.

Again the old man came out of his house. Holding on to another string, he followed it to a large woodpile and returned to the house with some wood. Soon Rabbit saw smoke coming from the chimney on the roof of the hut. He decided to go see what the old man was doing inside. He knocked on the door, and a weak old voice answered.

"Come on in," said the old man.

Rabbit saw that the old man was cooking dinner.

"Hello, sir," said Rabbit. "I have been on a long journey to find out about the world. This is a beautiful river that you live next to and a beautiful house you have to live in. You must have a nice time living here alone. I see that you have everything handy. You can get wood and water, but how do you get your food?" he asked.

"I am a powerful sorcerer," said the old man, "and when I need food I call to the fish who come to my pail, and the animals in the forest to bring me meat. The mice bring me rice and grain and the birds bring me leaves for my tea. But it is a hard life, for I am blind and I am all alone with no one to talk to."

Now Rabbit thought that being blind wasn't so bad if you can have all the food you want. So he said, "Old man, let us change places. I think I would like to live here."

"If we exchange my clothes for your rabbit-fur, you will become old and blind and I can live as you," said the old man.

"I don't care to be a rabbit anymore," said Rabbit. "Let us make the exchange."

Rabbit took the old man's clothes and gave him his own skin. As soon as they did this, the old man, now looking like a young rabbit, ran off laughing. Rabbit, in the old man's clothes, was left by himself and now he had become blind, just as the old man had been. He hadn't realized that he would become blind too.

Rabbit decided that he should get some more wood for the fire. He picked up one of the strings to guide himself. He bumped around the room and finally found the door. He walked a few steps, but then became confused. He wandered about, bumping against trees and finally tangling himself up in a big patch of thorn bushes. He was covered all over with scratches from his head to his toe. Then he began to cry out for his friend Wakan-Tanka.

Soon his friend appeared.

"What happened to you?" asked Wakan-Tanka.

"I made friends with an old sorcerer and I decided to see what it was like to live the way he did. But now I don't like it so much," replied Rabbit.

"Well, where is this old man?" asked Wakan-Tanka. "I don't see your new friend around anywhere."

"I don't know," said Rabbit. "I couldn't see which way he went."

"I will call the birds to help us find this man," said Wakan-Tanka.

Wakan-Tanka called all the birds and they came flying from every direction. As they arrived, Wakan-Tanka asked them if they had seen the old sorcerer, but none had. Finally the owl came. Wakan-Tanka asked him, "Have you seen the old man who lived here in this hut?"

"Hoo-hoo," replied owl.

"The old man who lived here."

"I did not see him," replied Owl, "but last night I saw a rabbit sleeping beneath a tree."

"Good for you, Owl," said Wakan-Tanka. "For this alert report I shall reward you. From now on only you will be able to hunt at night. The other birds, who are not as alert, will have to hunt during the heat of the day." Since that time the owl has been one of the few birds who are able to see and hunt during the dark of night.

Wakan-Tanka went into the woods and found the old man, who was still dressed in the skin of Rabbit. He brought him back to the hut. Wakan-Tanka was no longer patient with his friend Rabbit.

"I ought not to have helped you this time," he said. "Any one who is so dumb as to want to be someone else should be left without help. I am getting tired of your foolishness and will not help you next time."

Rabbit told Wakan-Tanka how sorry he was and promised to head for home. When he had nearly completed his journey, he came to a small creek. He took a long drink, for the trip had been a tiring one. While he was satisfying his thirst he heard some noise from a hill beside the creek. He looked up and saw four wolves struggling with each other. They were having a contest to test their strength. They were pulling each other this way and that with their tails intertwined.

"Let me pull tails with you," said Rabbit. "My tail is long and strong. This looks like fun."

"Come and join us," said the wolves, in a playful mood

They began to pull as hard as they could and before he realized it, Rabbit's tail was pulled right off.

"Wakan-Tanka! Wakan-Tanka! I have lost my tail!" cried Rabbit. "I need your help!"

Wakan-Tanka appeared out of nowhere. He looked at the pathetic rabbit and laughed.

"I warned you already, you silly rabbit," he said. "Anyway, you look better without a tail. Maybe it will remind you not to be so foolish."

From that time on rabbits have had no tails. In this way they are reminded not to take so many stupid chances.

From *Myths of the Sioux* by Marie L. McLaughlin, Bismarck Tribune Co. (1916)

OLD MAN AND THE BOBCAT

A Blackfoot Legend

After reading this story, many readers will be surprised to learn that Old Man is the chief god of the Blackfoot. He is their creator, who formed their world and its people, created their medicine and taught them which plants to use. He is the god of Algonquian-speaking tribes from the Atlantic to the Rocky Mountains. Yet he is not the all-powerful, all-knowing creator that Western cultures associate with the concept. He combines both strength and weakness; wisdom and foolishness; good and evil. Despite his power and wisdom, Old Man is often dependent on the advice of animals, yet he also will play tricks on them. It is believed among the Blackfoot that Old Man left them long ago, disappearing into the mountains to the West, but that he will return again to them someday.

Most people are familiar with western prairie dogs. They live in large communal towns which consist of individual burrows separated by approximately 50 feet of "home" territory for grazing. One advantage of living in these large groups is that if any one prairie dog sees danger approaching in the form of a coyote or other predator, all the others are instantly alerted by its barking, which gives the prairie dog its name. They are actually members of the squirrel family, closely related to chipmunks and woodchucks. Prairie dog towns may have as many as a thousand or more animals. In the past, there have been towns covering thousands of miles, with many millions of individuals. Because they compete with cattle for food, poisoning by ranchers has reduced their numbers, but not eliminated them. Since poisoning causes havoc among other wildlife as well, it is not considered to be a safe way of controlling problem animals. In the long run, encouraging a normal, healthy population of predators like the bobcat is a more effective control measure.

Since there are very few animals with short tails — among them bears, rabbits and bobcats —many native stories mention this unusual feature and how it was caused. Usually, the story involves some mischievous deed which causes the animal to be punished.

The bobcat is the most common and widespread of the wild cats to be found in North America. Not only has it survived the destruction of its habitat and unrestricted hunting much better than its relatives the lynx and cougar, but it actually has been expanding its range and can be found both in deep forests and in farm land in much of the United States. The bobcat is an efficient predator, and prairie dogs — among other small rodents — are a favorite food.

OLD MAN WAS TRAVELING AROUND THE PLAINS, WHEN HE SAW A BUNCH of prairie dogs sitting in a circle. They had built a fire and were sitting around it playing an odd sort of game. One of them would jump into the coals in the fire while the others covered him over with sand and ashes. When the buried prairie dog got too hot, he would yell out to the rest, "Quick, let me out!" and the others would uncover him as fast as they could.

Old Man asked, "Can I play your game too? I want to learn how to do that trick."

The prairie dogs were suspicious of Old Man at first because they knew that he was always up to some mischief. He finally convinced them to teach him this new game. They told him what to do, put him in the fire, and covered him up with the ashes. After a short while he would yell, just like the prairie dogs, and they would pull him out again. Then each of the prairie dogs would do the same and Old Man would help to get them out.

Finally, Old Man said, "Well, this has been fun, but let's try something different. This time I'll bury a whole bunch of you in the coals."

So they tried it that way, not suspecting that Old Man did not have very good intentions. He was really very hungry, and was trying to get an easy meal of cooked prairie dogs. When the buried prairie dogs started yelling, "Quick, it's getting too hot!" Old Man just ignored them.

When the rest of the prairie dogs realized what was happening, they quickly rushed to their dens. Nothing was about to stop Old Man from his dinner. He cut some willow branches on which to lay the feast and began to eat his catch. He ate until he was full, and then felt very sleepy. He said to his nose, "I am going to sleep now. I want you to keep alert, though. Watch for me and wake me if anything comes near."

Then the Old Man slept. Pretty soon his nose snored, waking him up. "What is it?" he asked.

The nose said, "A raven is flying over there."

"That is nothing," laughed Old Man, and went right back to sleep again. Soon his nose snored again. "What is it now?"

"There's a coyote over there, coming this way," said the watchful nose.

"A coyote is nothing to worry about," said Old Man, again falling asleep.

Soon nose snored again, but Old Man did not wake up this time. Again it snored and called out, "Quick, wake up. A bobcat is coming." But Old Man paid no attention. He just kept on sleeping.

Meanwhile the bobcat crept up to where the fire was, and ate up all the rest of Old Man's dinner. He then went off to a flat rock and lay down to digest his meal. All this time Old Man's nose kept trying to awaken him. Finally Old Man slowly came out of his sleep. "There's a bobcat over there on that flat rock. He has eaten all your food," his nose informed him.

Old Man was very angry. He went over to where the bobcat was and grabbed it before it could make a single move to scratch or bite him. The bobcat cried out, "Hold on, let me speak a word or two."

But Old Man would not listen. He said, "I will teach you a lesson for stealing my food." He pulled off the bobcat's tail and threw him high in the air. Bobcat came back down head first and quickly sneaked off into the brush. As he went away Old Man yelled after him, "There, that is the way you bobcats shall always be." And that is the reason why even today they have no tails and look as though they have had their faces pushed in.

From a Blackfoot legend collected by George Bird Grinnell, *Blackfoot Lodge Tales,* University of Nebraska Press, Lincoln (1962)

THE ORIGIN OF THE CHICKADEE

A Cree Folktale

The sounds that birds make to attract mates or defend territory are called songs, while other sounds they make are known as calls. Both males and females give various calls and sounds. This story tells how the chickadee came to be, along with the distinctive call from which it gets its name. The call, which has the repeated sound of "chick-a-dee-dee, chick-a-dee-dee-dee," is used when winter flocks become separated from each other or when one bird doesn't notice when the flock has moved on. The lost birds begin calling until they have made contact with the group and rejoined their brothers and sisters. In spring, when male chickadees establish territories and display for females, they whistle with their two-note mating call — "feebee, feebee." This is often used at other times of the year, with a whole series of high-pitched alarm, feeding and conflict calls associated with flock formation and communication. A winter flock of chickadees is usually made up of a dominant or leading pair which has successfully nested during the summer, along with its young and other paired and single adults. Other small birds, such as tufted titmice, nuthatches and downy woodpeckers, often join the chickadees as they visit feeding stations and search the woods for food. Mixed flocks enable the smaller birds more readily to detect attacks by predators such as hawks and cats.

IN THE FALL, WHEN THE LEAVES OF THE POPLAR AND THE BIRCH TREES ARE TURNING gold in color, the families of the Cree tribe go out on the lakes and rivers to their winter trapping grounds.

One family went to a certain place every year because it was plentiful in caribou, moose, muskrat, rabbit and beaver. Life was good for them in the winter months, and when the snow melted, the family would be sad because the best time of the year would be over.

One winter they had trapped many muskrat, beaver and rabbit and they did not know what they would do with all the meat. Soon spring would come and the family would not be able to take all that meat with them; they would have to leave it behind to rot. Since the father of this family did not want to waste their valuable food, he decided he would haul it to their summer lodge; but he could not take the meat and his two sons and daughter in one trip. So the father and mother decided to take most of the bundles and leave their children in the winter camp. They then would return to get them after they had brought the meat to their lodge.

The parents started on the journey to the summer home with the provender. The trail was still deep with snow and the trip took many more days than they expected. But the parents were not worried about their children because there was food for them to eat, and there was no danger from any animals such as wolves or bears.

A number of days after the parents had left, the boys awoke one frosty morning to discover that their little sister had wandered away from their campsite. They began to search for her in the forest, looking in her favorite hiding places, but not a trace of her could be found.

The boys wondered if the little girl had followed their parents, but they were afraid to go after their mother and father because they knew they were already a few days away. The boys were now very worried about their little sister. That night, as they sat by their campfire outside the lodge, they heard the sounds of wolves in the distance. This made them worry all the more. When it was completely dark, they went inside the lodge. They were very frightened, the more so when they heard the padded footsteps of animals outside. They also heard barking, howling and growling very close by. As the wolves came closer to the camp, the boys strung their bows and moved to the very back of the lodge, ready to protect themselves if the animals should enter. They stayed that way all night until the sun began to rise in the east.

The boys waited until the sun was full in the sky and then they went out of the lodge to look for their lost sister. They cried and cried for her, yelling her name "Chick-a-dee, Chick-a-dee," over and over. Suddenly the boys began to shrink in size and grow feathers. They were transformed into two tiny birds. The two birds flew into camp, where they began eating seeds that had been left out. They stayed there because plenty of food was available for them.

A few more days passed and the father came back to get his children. When he got close to camp he did not see any of them. He ran quickly to the lodge, but still no one was there. He listened for any sound of them, but he could not hear anything. Thinking that his children might be hiding, he started to look all around. Then he realized that something was wrong. After he searched many days for them, he finally gave up. He thought that his children might have been eaten by bears or some other ferocious animals. The father sat by the lodge, ill with sorrow. He then heard someone calling "Chick-a-dee, Chick-a-dee." He became excited because he thought it was his two sons. Then he saw two birds flying near him. He asked, "Little birds, why are you crying like that?"

The birds chirped, "Oh father, we have lost our little sister."

Then the birds started crying again and flew into the forest. This is why the chickadees call to each other when separated, as the two brothers did when searching for their lost little sister.

From a Cree legend collected by Carl Ray & James Stevens, *Sacred Legends of the Sandy Lake Cree*, McClelland & Stewart Ltd., Toronto (1971)

THE MALLARD'S TAIL

A Cree Folktale

The mallard drake or male is the only duck which possesses curled tail feathers, and this story is a Cree legend of how that came to be.

ONCE IN A CAMP CLOSE TO A GREAT SEA THERE LIVED A MAIDEN WHO WAS very much in love with a young brave in the same village. They met secretly in the evening to talk of their affection for each other. The young man wanted to take the maiden for his wife, but the chief of the village was against the marriage.

The girl had been promised to the chief many years before, when she was a small child. Now he told her parents that he would kill the maiden and her lover if they ever tried to marry. But the maiden continued to meet her lover. They decided to flee from the village so that the evil chief could not harm them.

They made their plans to escape one night and left telling no one where they were going. The young couple had not traveled very far before they heard something coming through the forest behind them. They began to run, fearing that it might be the angry chief trying to catch them and kill them.

They ran all night. The young brave backtracked, trying to throw the chief off their trail, but it was no use; towards morning they were still being followed, and were losing ground all the time. They appeared to be doomed because they had come to the shore of a great sea. They had taken the wrong trail somewhere and now they were trapped. There was no escape.

The young maiden began to cry because she knew her death would be horrible. The two lovers knelt in prayer, asking the greatest of all spirits to help them in this moment of terror. Behind them in the forest they could hear twigs and shrubs breaking as their fate approached them.

As they knelt there on the ground, they felt their bodies diminish in size. The couple thought that some evil had possessed them; they continued to weep. But as their bodies continued to shrink, feathers began to grow on them. Soon the maiden was covered with brown feathers and she cried to her lover, "We are to be saved, dear one." With that she flew up into the air.

By this time, the evil chief was very close. Just as he reached the young brave, now in the form of a male mallard, the chief grabbed at him, but caught only his tail feathers as he flew away to join his lover.

To the Cree people this explains how the mallards came to be living in this world, and why the drake has a curled tail.

From a Cree legend collected by Carl Ray & James Stevens, *Sacred Legends of the Sandy Lake Cree*, McClelland & Stewart Ltd., Toronto (1971)

Most of us are so familiar with the mallard that we might not notice something as subtle as the curled feathers of the tail. The next time you see a flock of mallards look for these. Also note the sound the drakes make. Only the females sound the familiar "quack," while males emit a nasal call which sounds like "rhaeb," as well as a variety of whistles. In springtime, the male mallard goes through a series of displays to attract a mate. Some of these movements are very subtle and last only a few seconds. Bobbing the head, tossing water in the air, shaking the bill and tail and preening in front of a female are some of the signs of mating activity. The males of most birds are more brightly colored than the females. This is part of selective evolution, which has favored the development of bright patterns and specialized feathers to enhance courtship displays. An extreme example of this kind of adaptation can be seen in the even larger tail feathers of the male pintail duck. The hen mallard, like most female ducks, is a mottled brown which provides better protection from predators, especially when sitting in her nest in a patch of marsh grass.

COYOTE IN THE CEDAR TREE

A Chinook Folkstory

Coyote is the animal form of the creator-god Old Man, who was often called Old Man Coyote. In some Northwest Indian tribes, the raven was considered to be the animal form of the Creator of man and the world. But whatever the animal used, the concept of the supernatural, magical being was the same. The coyote is an excellent personification of Old Man. Cunning, resourceful and intelligent, the coyote can live in areas that offer little food for larger predators. Coyotes eat mainly rabbits and rodents and have been able to take over much of the territory that was formerly occupied by their close relative the wolf. Coyotes are now found in most states, and live close to large cities. Hunting, poisoning and continued harrassment by human beings seem not to have affected them at all.

Most of the birds that Coyote summons for help in this story are not very good at chiseling holes in trees. Chickadees and nuthatches can dig holes in soft rotten wood, but only woodpeckers excel at excavating a hole for nesting. Even the larger birds with strong bills cannot make a dent in the cedar tree because their bills are constructed for tearing flesh, not for drilling holes. Many birds that commonly nest in holes — such as some flycatchers, tree swallows, purple martins, chickadees, house wrens, wood ducks, bluebirds and small owls —depend on the holes made by woodpeckers, since natural cavities are difficult to find. Woodpeckers have remarkable adaptations for their special foraging. They can perch vertically on the sides of trees, using their stiff tail feathers as support. Their skulls are much harder and thicker than those of other birds, and can really take a pounding. The larger of the two woodpeckers in this story is the pileated woodpecker, which can make cavities up to two feet in dead trees. Its name comes from a Latin word meaning "capped," referring to its bright red crest.

Coyote's enemy, the cougar, is the largest and most widespread of American cats, living from Canada all the way to the tip of South America. It was eliminated from the eastern part of the country by the advance of towns and cities and by the work of bounty hunters. Although the cougar avoids people, in the past it has been seen as a threat by those who did not understand its ways. Whereas the coyote pursues game until it can no longer run, the cougar or mountain lion is the master of stalking its prey. It slowly approaches to within twenty or thirty feet before it leaps after an animal. The cougar usually hunts deer, but often stalks smaller animals as well. Other than man, and coyotes with magical powers, the cougar has no natural enemies.

ONCE COYOTE WAS TRAVELING THROUGH THE MOUNTAINS, FOLLOWING a trail through the deep woods. As he was walking along looking for game, he saw an immense cedar tree. The inside was hollow. He could look into it through a big gap in the bark, but the hole was not big enough for him to crawl through. He thought that this would be a good hiding place from which to surprise game. So using his magical powers, he called out, "Open, cedar tree!" And the gap in the tree opened wider so that he could jump in.

Then he said, "Close, cedar tree!" and the gap closed again.

He stayed there awhile, but no game came by. He kept peeking out through the small gap, but he really wasn't able to see very much. Finally, he thought it was time to look someplace else.

"Open, cedar tree!" he said, but nothing happened.

"OPEN, CEDAR TREE!" he yelled, but still nothing happened. Coyote was very angry. He called to the tree; he kicked it. The tree did not answer. Then Coyote remembered that he was Coyote, the wisest and most cunning of all the animals. He began to think.

And after he thought for quite a while, he came up with a plan. He called all the birds to help him. He told them to peck a hole through the cedar tree. The first to try was Wren. Wren pecked and pecked at the tree until her beak was blunt. She did not even make a dent. Then Coyote called the other birds. Sparrow came, Robin came, Finch came, but none of them could break through the heavy bark.

Then Owl came, and Raven, and Hawk, and Eagle. They could not even make a little hole. Finally Downy Woodpecker came and made a small hole. Then the bigger Pileated Woodpecker landed on the side of the tree and positioned himself on the trunk, holding on with his long toes and strong tail feathers. He was able to peck a larger hole.

But still the hole was too small for Coyote to get out. He thanked all the birds for trying to help and wished them well. Coyote began to think hard again. Then after some time, he thought of another plan. Again using his magic powers, he began to take himself apart. He took himself all apart and slipped each piece through the hole that Woodpecker had made. First he slipped a leg through, then a paw, then his tail, then his ears, and his eyes, until he was all through the hole, and outside the cedar tree. Then Coyote began to put himself together. He put his legs and paws together, then his tail, his nose, his ears, and then

his body. At last Coyote had himself all together except for his eyes. He could not find his eyes. They had rolled somewhere down a hill, and without them he could not possibly find them.

Coyote did not want anyone to know he was blind, so he kept his eyelids shut tight and began to walk along the trail, feeling his way along. Soon he met Cougar, who was Coyote's enemy. Cougar began to jeer at Coyote.

"Oh, ho! You seem to be very blind, Coyote," he said. "If you could see, you would have run away from me a long time ago. No one lives very long who crosses my path."

"No, no," said Coyote. "I am walking like this for a special reason. I have trained my eyes to see the spirit world. Because I walk with my eyes shut tight, I am able to see things that no other animal can see. The lights of the spirit world show me where I can find food, so that I never have to hunt again. If you don't believe me, I will trade eyes with you."

Cougar was very excited about the idea of never needing to hunt for his meals. Unlike Coyote he did not like to have to run over miles and miles looking for food. Usually he would stay near one hiding spot and hope that game would come by. He quickly agreed to Coyote's trade, thinking he would keep the magic eyes for himself.

So Coyote and Cougar traded eyes, but when Coyote had eyes again he said, "Aha! I tricked you, Cougar. I have your eyes, but have none to give you. You won't be much good at hunting anymore. I will make it easy for you, though."

With that Coyote used his magic powers once more, and turned Cougar into a snail that creeps on the ground, searching for food.

From *Coyote Was Going There,* edited by Jarold Ramsey, University of Washington Press, Seattle (1977)